CYNTHIA RYLANT

Let's Go Home

THE WONDERFUL THINGS ABOUT A HOUSE

⚘ Illustrated by ⚘

WENDY ANDERSON HALPERIN

SIMON & SCHUSTER
BOOKS FOR YOUNG READE
NEW YORK   LONDON   TORONTO   S

SIMON & SCHUSTER BOOKS FOR YOUNG READERS

An imprint of Simon & Schuster Children's Publishing Division

1230 Avenue of the Americas, New York, NY 10020

SIMON & SCHUSTER BOOKS FOR YOUNG READERS

and colophon are registered trademarks of Simon & Schuster, Inc.

Also available in a Simon & Schuster Books for Young Readers hardcover edition.

Designed by Heather Wood

The text of this book was set in Italian Old Style.

Manufactured in China

First Aladdin Paperbacks edition October 2005

14 16 18 20 19 17 15

The Library of Congress has cataloged the hardcover edition as follows:

Rylant, Cynthia.

Let's go home : the wonderful things about a house / by Cynthia Rylant ;

illustrated by Wendy Anderson Halperin.—1st ed.

p. cm.

Summary: Describes the individual rooms in a house and what they mean to those who use them.

ISBN-13: 978-0-689-82326-8 (hc.)

ISBN-10: 0-689-82326-6 (hc.)

1. Dwellings—Juvenile literature. 2. Home—Juvenile literature. [1. Dwellings. 2. Home.]

I. Halperin, Wendy Anderson, ill. II. Title

TH4811.5R95 2000

392.3'6—dc21

99022574

ISBN-13: 978-1-4169-0839-5 (pbk.)

ISBN-10: 1-4169-0839-0 (pbk.)

0319 SCP

For our Lake Street home, with love

C . R .

To the character I found in the homes of artists
Fran and Terry Lacy, and Glen and Jackie Michaels
and
to the home Mary Rife created in the library
and
to Cynthia Rylant for the words to contemplate these places

W . A . H .

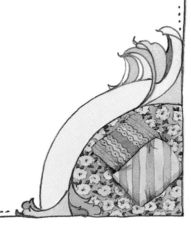

$\mathcal{T}$HERE ARE MANY kinds of houses in the world, from little cottages to big mansions, from farmhouses to bungalows.

But no matter the kind of house, it is the living inside that makes it wonderful, what happens in each room that makes it marvelous. It is what the house means to those who live there.

Let's walk through. Let's see the wonderful things about a house.

$\mathcal{I}$t is evening and the crickets are singing . . . let's go to the PORCH.
Cats love a front porch, and dogs do too. The cats will curl up by
a post and watch the birds in the garden or the bats in the sky.

Dogs usually stay on a rug somewhere near a chair, and the rug was probably put there just for them. The dogs try to sleep, but they never can. Something is always going on!

Often there are little visitors to a front porch. A wide raccoon with curious eyes may stop by. And bugs just love a porch at night when the light is on.

Of course, a front porch is never more beautiful than at Christmas.

Red and green lights curl up the posts, wind around the banisters, outline the door. And even the plainest little house will shine like a jewel in the night.

Oh, a front porch is a wonderful thing, but now let's step inside . . .

LIVING ROOMS are always so pretty. There is usually a big sofa, and it is meant to ask you to sit and stay awhile. In a living room that is exactly what people do.

In front of the sofa there is a coffee table, and it certainly has its name right, for coffee is often served here. But that isn't all. Some people love a

big bowl of nuts and some lemonade, and others love cold mugs of
milk with strawberry muffins, and a few just prefer the simplicity of
Japanese tea.

But whenever guests are here, always look *under* the coffee table too,
for the family dog is sure to be there with muffins in his eyes!

Some people are lucky enough to have a fireplace in their living room, and there are few things that make a person cozier. Husbands and wives who have been married a long time will put two matching

chairs near the fire, and they will spend the evening reading or sewing or simply being quiet together.

Few places are so friendly as a living room.

Ask anyone to name his favorite place in a house and he will almost always say the KITCHEN. It is because kitchens are so good to us. They have shiny red canisters full of rich dark coffee that smells like heaven,

and tidy white boxes of bread waiting for butter, and cheerful bowls of sugar that make everything taste better.

Kitchens are delicious.

Every kitchen has a refrigerator. Some are old and green and some are new and white. Some have a freezer on top and some have a freezer on the bottom (which dogs don't like, as their noses get frosty).

There's always a sink, of course, and a sink in front of the window is best of all, for the birds outside will visit at the feeder, and this can

make a person feel quite happy.

And if ever a kitchen is the most perfect place in the world to be, it is when cookies are being baked. White, fly-away flour is everywhere—on noses and fingers and hair. White-flour paw prints walk across the kitchen floor. And the smell of cookies makes every person as nice as he can be.

In a kitchen, people will pat each other on the back, give their
sweeties a hug, tuck a special treat in a little boy's lunch. It is the room
that reminds people to look after each other.

And when people are far away from home, feeling lonely and missing

things, often it is their sweet, wonderful kitchens they miss most of all.

And as soon as they come home, this is where they want to be, with a nice warm scone, and a cup of tea, and someone to kiss them kindly on the head.

$\mathcal{B}$elieve it or not, a BATHROOM can be the most interesting room in a house. In a bathroom you can find out what people like to read or how they like to smell or whether or not their teeth are real. Bathrooms are fun for kids and fun for grown-ups but not much fun for dogs. Dogs prefer the kitchen.

Children love the tub, of course. A little girl could spend an entire day in the tub with her toys if someone would let her. You can always tell if a child lives in a house by checking beside the tub. That's where you'll find the wind-up boats and the yellow ducky and the sponge that looks like a dinosaur.

What's nicest about bathrooms are the lovely things they have for people's bodies. Lavender soap or cinnamon oil or lotion that smells like oranges. Almond cream and peppermint rinse and hot pink polish for toes. Vanilla perfume and spice cologne and yellow banana for hair.

Bathrooms are always wonderful, personal, private little places in any house. Everyone leaves them relaxed and perfumed—and sometimes with a friendly dinosaur!

$\mathcal{B}$EDROOMS are important because they shelter us from the world like no other rooms can.

It is wonderful to be a child in bed on a cold winter morning and to hear your mother say the schools are closed because of snow. You snuggle in, all warm and happy, until you just can't bear it anymore.

Then up you jump, for there is *snow* out there! Good-bye, warm bed!
We write letters in our bedrooms and we read books in our bedrooms, but, best of all, we dream in our bedrooms. Sometimes we are wide-awake when we dream. We gaze at the oak tree outside the window and make wishes.

But the best dreams are sleep dreams where all of our wishes come true. Imagine all the houses in a little town at night and all the dreaming going on there! We leave the world to the deer and the owls and we dream. Then morning comes again and clothes are pulled on, shoes tied, beds made, kitties petted.

And away we go, out into the busy world of cars and trucks and school buses and grocery shopping and work in offices and work in yards and work in friendly little shops.

But at the end of every busy day, we know that a peaceful, quiet bedroom waits just for us. Waits for our dreams and plans.

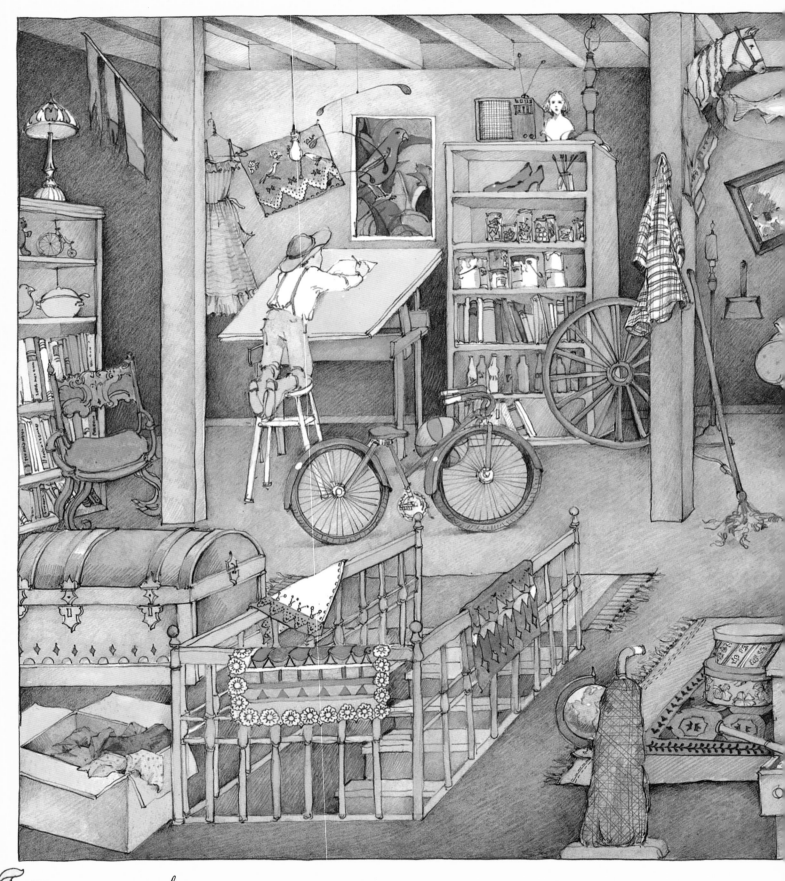

$\mathcal{A}$nd now that we have walked across the front porch and through the rooms of the house, there is still one more room left for us to explore: the ATTIC.

Attics are really beautiful. You can see the rafters of the house as they rise up to a point above you, and sometimes there will be a small attic window looking right out at the tops of trees. There may even be a

squirrel's nest there you never knew about.

Nearly every attic has a collection and some attics have *lots* of collections: comic-book collections and doll collections, coin collections and stamp collections. Some people are never quite sure what to do with the stuff they've collected, so up in the attic it goes!

Attics are filled with the past. And, for most people, the past is everything. An attic will hold the small box of baby things a mother has saved all these years: a lock of hair, a piece of blanket, a small bear with his nose kissed away.

This can be the wonderful thing about an attic: It can remind you of all the things you've done, and when you're finished thinking about the past, you can look out the window and think about all you want to do.

And when you come down from the attic, back into a house that is alive with smells from the kitchen and dogs barking and tubs running and doors opening and closing and opening again . . . you can breathe in the life of this wonderful house and be glad that for now it is yours.

Happy living.